Big Unicorn Feelings

Adapted by Maggie Testa
Based on the original book by Jessie Sima

Ready-to-Read

Simon Spotlight
New York   London   Toronto   Sydney   New Delhi

SIMON SPOTLIGHT
An imprint of Simon & Schuster Children's Publishing Division
1230 Avenue of the Americas, New York, New York 10020
This Simon Spotlight edition August 2024
DreamWorks Not Quite Narwhal © 2024 DreamWorks Animation LLC. All Rights Reserved.
All rights reserved, including the right of reproduction in whole or in part in any form.
SIMON SPOTLIGHT, READY-TO-READ, and colophon are registered trademarks of Simon & Schuster, LLC.
Simon & Schuster: Celebrating 100 Years of Publishing in 2024
For information about special discounts for bulk purchases, please contact
Simon & Schuster Special Sales at 1-866-506-1949 or business@simonandschuster.com.
Manufactured in the United States of America 0724 LAK
10 9 8 7 6 5 4 3 2 1
ISBN 978-1-6659-5846-2 (hardcover)
ISBN 978-1-6659-5845-5 (pbk)
ISBN 978-1-6659-5847-9 (ebook)

Kelp and his unicorn friends are playing rainbow tag.

But not Juniper.

She cannot make rainbows with her Unicorn Spark yet.

The unicorns play rainbow bubble tag and swishbee together.

Juniper feels left out.
"Grrr!" she says.

She takes the swishbee.

"Why did you do that?" asks Pixie.

Juniper does not know.

Leroy knows. He uses his Unicorn Spark to ask Juniper how she feels.

"Yes, I feel *angry*!" Juniper says.

"It is okay to feel how you feel," says Pixie.

"But it is not okay to take our swishbee."

What can make Juniper feel better?

"Dancing makes me feel good," says Kelp.

Juniper tries to dance, but she still feels angry.

Ollie says breathing in his sunny spot makes him feel good.

But Juniper still feels angry.

"Maybe a hug will help," says Pixie. Juniper hugs Pixie super tight.

She feels much better. But she hugs *too* tight. "Ouch!" says Pixie.

"It feels good to squeeze!" says Juniper.

But she cannot squeeze Pixie. What can she squeeze?

Leroy has an idea. She can squeeze his unicorn toy!

Juniper squeezes super hard.

She is not angry anymore!

"I am sorry," she says.

Juniper gives back the swishbee. They all play together!